CALICO ILLUSTRATED CLASSICS

Oscar Wilde's

THE PICTURE OF DORIAN GRAY

ADAPTED BY: Dotti Enderle
ILLUSTRATED BY: Eric Scott Fisher

magic
Wagon

visit us at www.abdopublishing.com

Published by Magic Wagon, a division of the ABDO Group,
8000 West 78th Street, Edina, Minnesota 55439. Copyright
© 2012 by Abdo Consulting Group, Inc. International copyrights
reserved in all countries. All rights reserved. No part of this
book may be reproduced in any form without written permission
from the publisher.

Calico Chapter Books™ is a trademark and logo of Magic Wagon.

Printed in the United States of America, Melrose Park, Illinois.
052011
092011
This book contains at least 10% recycled materials.

Original text by Oscar Wilde
Adapted by Dotti Enderle
Illustrated by Eric Scott Fisher
Edited by Stephanie Hedlund and Rochelle Baltzer
Cover and interior design by Abbey Fitzgerald

Library of Congress Cataloging-in-Publication Data

Enderle, Dotti, 1954-
  Oscar Wilde's The picture of Dorian Gray / adapted by Dotti
Enderle ; illustrated by Eric Scott Fisher.
       p. cm. -- (Calico illustrated classics)
  Summary: An incredibly handsome young man in Victorian England
retains his youthful appearance over the years while his portrait
reflects both his age and evil soul as he pursues a life of decadence
and corruption.
  ISBN 978-1-61641-618-8
  [1. Conduct of life--Fiction. 2. Supernatural--Fiction. 3. Portraits--
Fiction. 4. London (England)--History--1800-1950--Fiction. 5. Great
Britain--History--Victoria, 1837-1901--Fiction.] I. Fisher, Eric Scott,
ill. II. Wilde, Oscar, 1854-1900. Picture of Dorian Gray. III. Title. IV.
Title: Picture of Dorian Gray.
  PZ7.E69645Os 2011
  [Fic]--dc22   2011010664

Table of Contents

THE PORTRAIT

The studio was filled with the rich odor of roses. And when the wind stirred, the heavy scent of lilacs filled the room. In the center of the room, clamped to an easel, stood the portrait of handsome young man.

The studio belonged to an artist named Basil Hallward. He'd been working on this special portrait and invited his friend Lord Henry Wotton over for a look. Lord Henry gazed at the picture with a smile.

"My, my," he said. "It is your best work, Basil. You must send it over to the Academy. Everything is so dull there."

"I don't think I shall send it there," Basil said, tossing his head back. "No, I won't send it anywhere."

"Not send it anywhere? Why not?" Henry couldn't believe it. "You artists are odd fellows. You want to gain fame, but when you have the chance, you throw it away. That's so silly. There is only one thing in the world worse than being talked about, and that is not being talked about. A portrait like this would set you high above all the young artists in England."

"I know you will laugh at me," Basil replied, "but I really can't display this portrait to the public. I've put too much of myself into it."

Lord Henry relaxed on the sofa and laughed. "Too much of yourself? You look nothing like the man in this portrait. You are rugged with coal-black hair. This young man is golden blond with fair skin."

"You don't understand, Harry," the artist said. "Of course I am not like him. I know that perfectly well. But you would not understand. You have wealth. I have artistic talent. And Dorian Gray has his good looks. We may all suffer from them."

"Dorian Gray? Is that his name?" asked Lord Henry, walking across the studio.

"Yes," Basil replied.

Lord Henry stared at the portrait with intrigue. "And where did you meet Dorian Gray?"

"The story is simple," the painter said. "Two months ago I attended a party at Lady Brandon's estate. You know we poor artists must show ourselves in society from time to time. I was there about ten minutes when I had the feeling that someone was watching me. I turned halfway around and saw Dorian Gray for the first time. I knew right off that he was a fascinating person, yet I felt a chill of fear. But once Lady Brandon introduced us, we became friends at once."

Lord Henry nodded. "And you see him often?"

"Nearly every day, now that I'm painting his portrait. He has inspired me. Because of him, I am a better artist."

"I must meet him," Lord Henry exclaimed.

Basil was reluctant. "I don't want you to meet him."

"You don't want me to meet him?"

"No," Basil said.

But it was too late. The butler entered, saying, "Mr. Dorian Gray is here, sir."

"You have to introduce me now!" cried Lord Henry, laughing.

The painter turned to the butler, who stood blinking in the sunlight. "Ask Mr. Gray to wait a few moments."

The man bowed and left.

Basil turned to Lord Henry. "Dorian Gray is my dearest friend," he said. "Please don't be a bad influence on him. My art has improved since I met Dorian. Please don't do anything to hurt that."

"Nonsense," said Lord Henry, smiling. Then he led Basil from the studio.

CHAPTER 2

YOUTH AND BEAUTY

As they entered the music room, they saw Dorian Gray. He was seated at the piano, looking over some of the sheet music.

"You must lend me some of these, Basil," he cried. "I want to learn to play them. They are perfectly charming."

"Well," Basil teased, "that depends on how well you pose today."

"I'm tired of sitting and posing. And I don't want a life-sized portrait of myself," he said as he spun around on the music stool. His cheeks blushed when he saw Lord Henry standing there. "I beg your pardon, Basil. I didn't know you had anyone with you."

"This is Lord Henry Wotton," Basil said. "He's an old Oxford friend of mine. I have been telling him what a patient art subject you are. Now you've spoiled it."

Henry stepped forward and extended his hand. "You have not spoiled anything, Mr. Gray. It is my pleasure to meet you. My aunt, Lady Agatha, has often spoken of you. You are one of her favorites."

"I'm afraid Lady Agatha is upset with me at present," Dorian said. "I promised to go to the club with her last Tuesday and completely forgot."

"Don't worry," Lord Henry told him. "She'll forgive you. She likes you very much."

Lord Henry looked at Dorian, thinking he was very handsome with his blue eyes and gold hair. And there was something in his face that made you trust him right away.

The painter set about mixing his colors and getting his brushes ready. He looked worried. "Harry," Basil said to Lord Henry, "would you think I was being rude if I asked you to go away?"

Lord Henry turned to Dorian. "Do you want me to leave?" he asked.

"No, I'd like you to stay. Besides, Basil is in one of his bad moods. I don't like being with him when he acts this way."

"Fine," Basil said. "If Dorian wishes you to stay, then you must stay."

But Lord Henry picked up his hat and gloves. "I really should be going anyway. I am meeting someone later. Mr. Gray, come and see me some afternoon. I am nearly always at home at five o'clock. Let me know ahead of time when you're coming."

"Basil," cried Dorian Gray, "if Lord Henry goes, then I go too. You are always so quiet when you paint. It gets so boring around here. Please ask him to stay."

Basil let out a sigh. "Have a seat, Harry. It seems Dorian wants you here."

Lord Henry watched as Basil painted. "The gods have been good to you, Dorian. You are young and handsome. Youth is so important."

"I don't think so," Dorian said.

"You only have a few years of youth before it's taken away. And then your beauty goes with it. When you're old, wrinkled, and ugly, you'll change your mind. You'll think it is very important. Make the most of your youth. Live life fully. Look for excitement! When you're young, the world is yours. There is absolutely nothing better in the world than youth."

Dorian Gray listened, open-eyed and wondering.

"There you have it. Aren't you glad you met me?" Lord Henry asked.

"I'm very glad," Dorian replied.

"Then let us always be friends."

It was then that Basil announced, "It is finished."

Lord Henry stepped over to admire the portrait. "My goodness!" he exclaimed. "This is your finest work, Basil!"

Dorian took a look, then drew back. Joy filled his eyes. The portrait showed all his splendid youth and beauty. He stood, gazing at it, and thinking of what Lord Henry had said. One day he would be old and wrinkled, his eyes dim and colorless.

"Don't you like it?" cried Basil, stung by Dorian's silence.

"Of course he likes it," said Lord Henry. "Who wouldn't like it? It is one of the greatest pieces of modern art. How much do you want for it? I must have it."

"It is not my property, Harry," Basil answered. "It belongs to Dorian."

"He is a very lucky fellow."

"How sad it is," murmured Dorian, his eyes still fixed on his portrait. "How sad it is! I shall grow old and horrible and dreadful. But this picture of me will always remain young. It will never be older than it is this minute. If only it could be the other way around. I wish I could stay young and the picture would grow old. For that I would give anything! I would even give my soul!"

"I don't think Basil would like that," Lord Henry said. "It would wrinkle his wonderful painting."

"Yes," Basil teased. "I would strongly object."

Dorian Gray turned and looked at him. "I believe you would. You like your art better than your friends."

The painter stared in amazement. What had happened? Why did Dorian seem so angry?

"You will always love your paintings and sculptures," Dorian went on, "but how long will you like me? Just until I get my first wrinkle, I suppose. I know now that when my good looks are gone, I'll lose everything. No one will care about me. Your picture has taught me that. Lord Henry is right. Youth is the only thing worth having."

Lord Henry turned pale and caught his hand. "Dorian! Don't talk like that. I have never met anyone like you. You shall always be my friend."

"So," said Basil, "it seems as though you hate the portrait. Then I shall destroy it." He searched through his artist tools and selected a small knife. It was just right for slicing the canvas.

"Don't, Basil!" Dorian cried. "That would be murder!"

"I'm glad you finally appreciate my work," Basil said to him.

"Appreciate it? Basil, I'm in love with it. I feel that it is a part of me," Dorian assured him.

"Once it is dry," Basil said, "you can take it home."

SIBYL VANE

At twelve thirty the next day, Lord Henry Wotton strolled from Curzon Street over to the Albany Club to see his uncle, Lord Fermor. When Lord Henry entered, he found his uncle sitting and grumbling over an article in the newspaper.

"Well, Harry, what brings you out so early?" his uncle asked. "I thought you young gentlemen slept until two and were not seen until five."

"I'm up early to see you," Lord Henry answered. "I need something."

"Money, I suppose," Lord Fermor said, making a sour face. "Young people nowadays think money is everything."

"No," Henry answered, "I don't want money, Uncle George. What I want is information."

"What information?" his uncle asked.

"I want to ask you about Dorian Gray."

"Who is he?" asked Lord Fermor, knitting his bushy white eyebrows.

"That's what I'm hoping to find out. I know that he is the last grandson of Lord Kelso. His mother was Lady Margaret Devereaux. I want you to tell me about her. What was she like?"

"Kelso's grandson!" the old gentleman bellowed. "Of course! I knew his mother. She was a beautiful girl. She could've married any young man she wanted, but she ran away with a penniless young fellow. A mere nobody.

"Sadly, the poor chap was killed in a duel a few months after the marriage. They said Kelso was behind it all. He paid some brute to insult his son-in-law in public, knowing they would settle it with pistols. It was all hushed up though.

"Kelso brought his daughter home, but she never spoke to him again. She died within a year, but she left behind a son. They were rich people, Harry. Dorian Gray will inherit quite a bit of money one day."

"Thank you for the information, Uncle," Lord Henry said. He bid Lord Fermor good-bye.

Lord Henry left, thinking about the story of Dorian's parents. What a strange romance. A beautiful woman risking everything for passion and only granted a few weeks of happiness. What agony she must have suffered. And poor Dorian left to be raised by his cranky old grandfather. Behind every wonderful thing that existed is something tragic.

But Lord Henry decided right then that he'd be the best friend Dorian ever had. He would always be there for him, no matter what.

A month later, Dorian Gray was sitting in the library at Lord Henry's house. Lord Henry had not yet come in. It seemed he was always late. Dorian thumbed through the pages of a book while he waited.

At last he heard footsteps outside, then the door opened. "I'm glad you're finally here, Harry," Dorian said.

"I'm afraid it's not Harry," answered a shrill voice.

Dorian quickly glanced around and rose to his feet. "I'm sorry. I thought—"

"I am Lord Henry's wife, Victoria. And I know who you are because I've seen pictures of you. Harry has many photographs."

"It is a pleasure to meet you, Lady Henry."

"It is a pleasure to meet you," she said. "You and Harry seem to be great friends."

It was then that Lord Henry entered. "So sorry I'm late, Dorian. I went to look for an old piece of fabric and had to bargain for it for hours. Nowadays people know the price of everything and the value of nothing. Ah! I see you've met my wife."

"She's a delightful woman," Dorian said.

Lady Henry smiled. "I was anxious to meet Mr. Gray, but now I must be going. I have promised to visit the Duchess. Good-bye, Mr. Gray. Good-bye, Henry."

Lady Henry flitted out of the room, and Lord Henry sat down on the sofa. He said, "Never marry a woman with red hair, Dorian."

"Why not?"

"Because they are so sentimental. I would advise that you never marry at all," Lord Henry said.

"But Harry, I have fallen in love," Dorian informed him.

"Who are you in love with?" Lord Henry asked, after a pause.

"With an actress," said Dorian, blushing.

Lord Henry was now filled with curiosity. "Who is she?"

"Her name is Sibyl Vane."

"I've never heard of her," Lord Henry said.

"No one has," Dorian said. "But everyone will someday. She is a genius."

"How long have you known her?" Lord Henry asked.

"About three weeks."

"And how did you meet her?"

"Harry, you have always encouraged me to seek adventure. So one evening I was exploring London and came across an odd little theater with flaring gaslights. A man out front invited me in. I'm not sure why I decided to enter, but I'm so glad I did," Dorian said.

"The play was *Romeo and Juliet*. Romeo was played by an elderly gentleman with thick eyebrows and a husky voice. But then I saw Juliet! She had dark brown hair, violet eyes, and such beauty as you've never seen.

"I was invited backstage to meet her. Sibyl was so shy and so gentle. And she called me Prince Charming."

Lord Henry sat back, observing his friend. "Indeed you are in love."

"And you and Basil must come with me to the theater tomorrow night to see her act. She will be playing Juliet again. Then you will see what a genius she is."

"Very well," Lord Henry said. "Tomorrow night. But now, I must leave. Good-bye, Dorian."

The next day Lord Henry sat at home, thinking of his friend. What would happen to Dorian? Was he really in love with the actress? His questions were answered when a telegram arrived. It was from Dorian. He and Sibyl were now engaged to be married.

A Promise

"Mother, Mother, I am so happy!" whispered Sibyl Vane.

Her mother was a tired-looking woman. She sat in a ragged arm chair, listening to her daughter.

"I am so happy!" Sibyl repeated. "And you must be happy, too!"

Mrs. Vane winced. "I am only happy when I see you act. You must not think of anything but your acting. Your manager, Mr. Isaacs, has been good to us. And we owe him money."

The girl looked up and pouted. "What does money matter? Love is more important than money."

"Mr. Isaacs has loaned us a large sum of money, Sibyl. He has been most considerate."

Sibyl walked over and sat in the window seat. "But he is not a gentleman. I hate the way he talks to me."

"I don't know how we would get by without him," her mother said.

Sibyl Vane tossed her head and laughed. "We don't need him anymore, Mother. Prince Charming will take care of us. I am so in love with him."

"My child, you are far too young to think of falling in love. You haven't known this gentleman very long. You can't know that much about him!" Mrs. Vane said.

"Please, Mother, let me be happy!"

It was then that the door opened and James Vane, Sibyl's brother, came into the room. Both Sibyl and her mother were pleased to see him.

James had overheard the conversation. He looked into his sister's face with tenderness. "I want you to take a walk with me in the park. I'm leaving for Australia tomorrow, so this is our last chance. I don't suppose I'll ever see London again."

"Let me change my clothes," Sibyl said. "Only the finest-dressed people go to the park."

"Don't be long," he called to her as she hurried upstairs.

James paced the room, then turned to his mother. "Are my things ready?"

"Yes, Jim," his mother answered. "But I wish you would stay. You could work as a clerk in a law office."

"I hate offices," he replied. "I have chosen the life I want. But please watch over Sibyl. Don't let her come to any harm."

"Of course I will watch over her."

"I hear a young gentleman comes to the theater every night to see her. Is that true?"

"Yes," his mother answered. "She says he is a fine gentleman. And if he is wealthy, he'd make a good husband for her."

James muttered something to himself as he drummed on the window pane with his coarse fingers. He had just turned around to say something when the door opened and his sister ran in.

"Let's go, Sibyl," he said to her.

The siblings went out into the flickering, wind-blown sunlight and strolled down dreary Euston Road. People passing by glanced at them in wonder. They made an odd-looking couple—a burly young man and a graceful girl. They looked like a gardener and a rose.

Sibyl was unaware of the effect she was producing. She was only thinking of her Prince Charming. James broke the silence by saying, "You have a new friend, I hear. Who is he? Why have you not told me about him? I think he's no good for you!"

"Stop, Jim!" she exclaimed. "You must not say anything against him. I love him."

"But you've known him for such a short time," said James. "Who is he? I have a right to know."

"I call him Prince Charming. Don't you like the name? If you saw him, you would think he's the most wonderful person in the world. Someday you'll meet him. Everybody likes him. I wish you could come to the theater tonight. He will be there. How wonderful it is to be in love and play Juliet!"

"So he is a gentleman?" James asked.

"A prince!" she cried musically.

"I want you to beware of him, Sibyl. And I promise, if he ever hurts you, I shall kill him."

CHAPTER 5

HORRID CRUELTY

"I suppose you've heard the news, Basil," Lord Henry said that evening at dinner.

"No, Harry," answered the artist. "What is it? Nothing about politics, I hope. It doesn't interest me."

"Dorian Gray is engaged to be married," said Lord Henry, watching him as he spoke.

Basil frowned. "Dorian is engaged to be married! Impossible!"

"It is perfectly true."

"To whom?" Basil asked.

"To some unknown actress."

Basil shook his head. "I can't believe it. Dorian is far too sensible."

"Dorian is far too wise not to do foolish things now and then, my dear Basil."

"Marriage is hardly a thing that one does now and then, Harry."

"But I didn't say he was married," said Lord Henry. "I said he was engaged to be married. There is a big difference."

"But think of Dorian's birth and position and wealth," Basil went on. "It would be absurd for him to marry a girl beneath his own class."

"If you want him to marry this girl, Basil, then tell him. He is sure to do it then."

"I just hope the girl is good, Harry. I'd hate to see Dorian tied to some vile creature who would weaken his nature and ruin his intellect."

"She is better than good. Dorian says she is beautiful," murmured Lord Henry. "He is not often wrong about things like that. But don't worry. We are to meet her tonight if that boy doesn't forget his appointment."

"Do you approve of the marriage?" Basil asked, biting his lip. "Surely you don't approve."

"It doesn't matter if I do or not. Dorian has a mind of his own."

Dorian walked in, flushed with excitement and pleasure. He shook hands with both his friends.

"Harry, Basil, you must both congratulate me!" he declared. "I have never been so happy. I know it is sudden, but all really delightful things are. It seems I have been looking for love like this all my life."

"I hope you will always be very happy," Basil said.

"Come have dinner with us, Dorian," Lord Henry said. "You can tell us all about the engagement."

"There isn't much to tell," Dorian informed them. "I went back to the theater last night to watch her act. She played the part of Rosalind. You should have seen her! She is simply a born artist.

"I went backstage to see her, and as we were sitting together, my lips moved to hers and we kissed. She said she was not worthy to be my wife. Not worthy! The whole world is nothing to me without her."

"It sounds as though you love her very much," Basil said.

"Yes. I am different around her. I would never treat her badly. Any man that would is a beast. A beast without a heart! I wish I could place her on a pedestal of gold so the whole world could see the woman I adore. She makes me a better person."

"Then I can't wait to meet her," Basil said.

After dinner, the three men put on their coats and took a carriage to the theater.

For some reason, the run-down theater was very crowded that night. A fat man with lots of jeweled rings on his hands led them to their seats.

"What a crude place," Lord Henry said, gesturing to the loud, rude audience.

"Yes," Dorian agreed, "but the common, rough people here will be quite different when Sibyl takes the stage. They all sit silently to watch her. Her acting is so good they laugh when she does. They weep when she does. She has them under her spell."

"Don't worry about anything Harry says," Basil told Dorian. "Anyone you love must be marvelous."

"Thank you, Basil," Dorian said.

Soon Sibyl stepped onto the stage. She was certainly lovely to look at—one of the loveliest creatures Henry had ever seen. She was shy and graceful with a faint blush on her cheeks.

But when it came time to speak, Sibyl was dull and listless. Her words sounded artificial. Her acting was terrible.

Dorian grew pale as he watched her. He was puzzled and anxious. Neither of his friends spoke. Dorian knew they were horribly disappointed.

The audience became bored. They yelled and whistled and hissed.

After the second act, Lord Henry put on his coat. "She is quite beautiful," he said to Dorian, "but she can't act. I think we should leave."

"I am going to wait until it's over," Dorian said in a hard, bitter voice. "I am awfully sorry that I made you waste an evening, Harry. I apologize to you both."

"Come, Basil," Lord Henry said. "Let us go."

Dorian sat through the entire play. When it was finished, he went back to see Sibyl. He needed an explanation.

Sibyl stood with a look of triumph on her face. When she saw him, an expression of joy came over her.

"How bad was my acting?" she asked.

"Horrible!" Dorian answered, gazing at her in amazement. "It was dreadful. Are you ill?"

"I shall never act well again," she informed him. "I shall always be a bad actress."

He shrugged his shoulders. "You were ridiculous. My friends were bored. I was bored."

She seemed not to listen to him. "Before I knew you, acting was the only real thing in my life—the only joy. But you came along and taught me what reality is. Oh, my Prince Charming, you are more to me than acting. Take me away with you. I hate the theater. I love only you."

Dorian flung himself down on a sofa and turned his face away. "You have killed all the love I had for you," he muttered.

She walked over to him and stroked his hair. She knelt down and pressed his hands to her lips, but he drew them back.

He leaped up and went to the door. "Yes," he cried, "you have killed my love! I loved you because you were marvelous, but you have thrown it all away. You are nothing to me now. I never want to see you again!"

The girl grew white and trembled. "You can't be serious," she murmured. "You must be acting."

"Acting!" he cried. "I'll leave that to you."

Dorian turned and left the room. In a few moments he was out of the theater. He wandered through the dimly lit streets, past black-shadowed archways and evil-looking houses. At dawn he hailed a hansom cab and drove home.

As he turned the handle on his door, Dorian saw the portrait that Basil had painted of him. He started back in surprise. The face appeared to have changed. The expression looked different. There was a touch of cruelty around the mouth. It was eerily strange.

What is happening? Dorian examined the picture. There were deep lines of cruelty around the lips as though he had done something horrible. He took a look at his own reflection, but the lines weren't there. They were only in the portrait.

He threw himself down in a chair to think. Suddenly it flashed across his mind. Yes, he remembered it perfectly. He had uttered a mad wish that he could remain young and the picture would grow old. Had his wish been fulfilled? But that's impossible! But it was there. He could see it.

Dorian had been cruel to Sibyl. That must be the answer. But he was too selfish to worry about that. He was more concerned about what would happen to the painting. Every time he committed a sin, its beauty would fade.

Dorian decided he would never sin again. And he would have to repair his relationship with Sibyl. He would go back tomorrow night and ask her to marry him. They would be happy again.

He got up from his chair and drew a large screen in front of the portrait. He couldn't look at it.

"How horrible!" he murmured to himself. Then he stepped outside, thinking only of his future bride.

CHAPTER 6

TERRIBLE NEWS

It was long past noon when Dorian woke up. His valet, Victor, came in with a cup of tea and the morning mail. Dorian sorted through the letters and saw there was one from Lord Henry. He tossed it aside to read later. The others were a boring assortment of cards, dinner invitations, and tickets to charity events.

As soon as he was dressed, he went into the library and sat down for a light breakfast. It was a beautiful day, and he felt perfectly happy. Suddenly his eye fell to the screen he'd placed in front of the portrait. Was it true? Had the portrait really changed? Maybe it had been his imagination.

Dorian got up and locked the doors. Then he moved the screen aside. It was true! The

portrait had definitely changed. He simply
could not believe it. But there it was, right in
front of him.

He shuddered as he walked back to his chair.
He'd never been so frightened. He gazed at
the picture with sickened horror. It made him
realize how cruel he'd been to Sibyl.

Dorian sat for a few more hours, worried
and confused. At half past four, he went over
to the table and wrote a letter to Sibyl. He
wrote page after page of how sorry he was.

He begged for her forgiveness. And just as he finished, there was a knock on the door. He heard Lord Henry call out, "Dorian, let me in. I must see you at once."

Dorian jumped up and covered the portrait with the screen, then he unlocked the door.

"I'm so sorry about what happened," Lord Henry said as he entered.

"Do you mean about Sibyl Vane?" Dorian asked.

"Yes, of course," Lord Henry answered, sinking into a chair. "It's dreadful, but surely it was not your fault. Did you go back to see her after the play?"

"Yes."

"And did you quarrel?"

"I was brutal, Harry. But it's all right now. I am sorry for everything that's happened between us. It has taught me a lesson."

"I am so glad you feel that way. I thought you'd be in agony."

"I'm fine now," Dorian said, shaking his head. "I am perfectly happy. And I am still going to marry Sibyl."

"Marry Sibyl?" cried Lord Henry, standing up and looking at him in amazement. "Didn't you get my letter? I wrote to you this morning."

"No, I haven't read it yet."

Lord Henry walked across the room and sat next to Dorian. "My letter was to tell you that Sibyl is dead."

Dorian leaped to his feet. "It can't be true!"

"It is quite true. It is in all the morning papers. She was leaving the theater with her mother, then said she'd forgotten something upstairs. Her mother waited and waited, but Sibyl did not come down. Later they found her lying on the floor of her dressing room. She had swallowed some poison and died instantly."

"Harry, this is dreadful! I have murdered Sibyl as surely as if I had cut her little throat with a knife. I was terribly cruel to her."

"I'm sure it was not your fault, Dorian. Don't blame yourself," Lord Henry said. "Remember, you have your whole life ahead of you. With your good looks, there is nothing that you will not be able to do."

But Dorian was not so sure. After a few more words of encouragement, Lord Henry said good-bye.

Once he had left, Dorian rushed over to the screen and drew it back. Had the lines of cruelty appeared the moment Sibyl drank the poison?

A feeling of pain crept over him. He thought of praying that the connection between him and the portrait might cease. But he didn't pray. He wanted to stay young forever. And he smiled a little as he drew the screen back in front of the picture.

THE HIDDEN PORTRAIT

The next day, Basil Hallward came to see him. "I read about what happened in the newspaper. I can't tell you how heartbroken I am over the whole thing. Did you go down to see the girl's mother?"

"No," answered Dorian. "I was at the opera."

"You went to the opera?" Basil said with pain in his voice. "You went to the opera while Sibyl Vane lay dead?"

"Stop, Basil! I won't hear anymore," Dorian cried, leaping to his feet. "What is done is done."

"Dorian, this is horrible! I don't know what has come over you," Basil declared.

Dorian got up and went to the window. He stood, gazing out at the lush, green garden.

After a few moments, Basil said, "Well, Dorian, I won't speak of this again. But I would like you to do something for me. I want you to come and sit for another portrait."

"I can't, Basil. It is impossible."

The painter stared at him. "My dear boy, what nonsense. Do you not like the portrait I painted for you?"

That's when Basil noticed the screen in front of it. "Why is it hidden? Show it to me." He walked toward it.

A cry of terror broke from Dorian Gray's lips. He rushed between the painter and the screen.

"Basil," he said, looking very pale, "you must not look at it."

"Not look at my own work? You are not serious. Why shouldn't I look at it?" asked the painter, laughing.

"If you try to look at it, I will never speak to you again."

Basil was thunderstruck. He looked at Dorian with amazement. He had never seen him like this before. Dorian was trembling all over.

"Dorian, what is the matter? It's absurd that I can't see my own work. Especially since I was planning to exhibit it in Paris."

"You want to exhibit it?" exclaimed Dorian, a strange sense of terror creeping over him. Was the world going to see his secret? No! Something had to be done.

"Yes," said Basil. "And if you're keeping it behind a screen, you can't care much for it."

Dorian passed his hand over his forehead. There were beads of sweat there. He felt he was on the brink of horrible danger.

"You told me that you would never exhibit it!" he cried. "What reason did you have for refusing to exhibit it before?"

The painter shuddered in spite of himself. "Dorian, you would only laugh at me if I told you. If you don't want me to look at our picture again, I won't. Your friendship is more important to me."

"No, Basil, you must tell me," Dorian insisted. "I think I have a right to know." His feeling of terror was replaced with curiosity. He had to find out Basil's secret.

"Let us sit down, Dorian," said the painter, looking troubled. "And just answer me one question. Have you noticed something curious about the picture? Something that didn't strike you at first, but revealed itself suddenly?"

"Basil!" cried Dorian, clutching the arms of his chair with trembling hands. He gazed at him with wild, startled eyes.

"I see you did. Don't speak. Wait until you hear what I have to say. From the moment I met you, Dorian, your personality has greatly influenced me. One day, a fatal day, I decided to paint a wonderful portrait of you as you really are.

"Whether it was the realism of the method or the wonder of your personality, I'm not sure. But I worked very hard and put so much of myself into it. I was afraid people would look at the picture and know how much I praised you. That is why I didn't want to exhibit it."

Basil paused, then said, "It's extraordinary to me that you have seen the same thing in the portrait. Did you really see it?"

"I saw something in it," he answered, "something that seemed to me very curious."

"Well, you don't mind my looking at it now?"

Dorian shook his head. "You must not ask me that, Basil. I could not possibly let you stand in front of that picture."

"But you will someday?"

"Never."

"Well, perhaps you are right. And good-bye for now, Dorian. You have been the one person in my life who has really influenced my art. I hope you will sit for me again."

"Impossible! I can't explain it to you, Basil, but I must never sit for you again. There is something mysterious about a portrait. It has a life of its own."

"I understand," Basil said. Then the two men said their good-byes.

Dorian smiled to himself. Poor Basil! He did not know the truth. Dorian had succeeded in keeping his secret. But he could not risk someone discovering it. The portrait must be hidden away!

THE LIFE OF DORIAN GRAY

Dorian called for his housekeeper, Mrs. Leaf. After a few moments, she bustled in. He asked her for the key to the old schoolroom.

"The old schoolroom, Mr. Dorian?" she asked. "Why, it is full of dust. I must clean it up before you go into it. It is not fit for you to see, sir."

"I don't want it cleaned up, Leaf. I only want the key," Dorian said.

"Well, sir, you'll be covered in cobwebs if you go into it. Why, it hasn't been opened for nearly five years."

"That does not matter," he said. "I simply want to see the place. Give me the key."

"Here is the key, sir," said the old lady. "But you aren't thinking of living up there, are you?"

"No, no," he cried. "Thank you, Leaf. That will do."

Mrs. Leaf lingered for a moment, then left. As the door closed, Dorian put the key in his pocket and looked around the room. His eye fell on a seventh-century purple cloth that his grandfather had found in a convent in Italy. Yes, that would serve as a wrap to hide the dreadful thing. It had been used to wrap the dead. Now it would wrap something much worse!

It was five o'clock when Dorian went into his library. His eye fell to a little yellow book that Lord Henry had sent him. *What is it?* he wondered. He flung himself into an armchair and turned through the pages. It was the strangest book that he had ever read.

It was a novel without a plot. It only had one character, a young Parisian man who spent his life in the nineteenth century trying to realize the passions of every century before. It was an evil book! But Dorian could not put it down. He read on and on until late at night.

For years, Dorian could not free himself from the book. But he never tried. He ordered nine copies from Paris and had them bound in different colors to suit his many moods.

The hero of the book, the wonderful young Parisian, was much like Dorian himself. The whole book seemed to contain the story of his own life before he had even lived it! The book changed Dorian forever.

Basil had captured Dorian's true beauty in his portrait. That is why people who heard awful rumors about Dorian refused to believe them. No one as young and handsome as Dorian could have done the awful things that were being whispered about him. And he appeared to be a man who kept to himself.

Dorian would often spend time away on some long, mysterious journey. And when he'd return, he would creep upstairs to the locked room and open the door with the key that he always kept with him.

He would stand in front of a mirror and compare his image with the one in the portrait. His face in the picture looked evil and aged compared to the fair, young face that laughed back at him from the mirror. He grew more and more taken with his own beauty, and more and more interested in the corruption of his own soul.

Dorian secretly spent time at a rough, filthy tavern near the docks. He wore a disguise and used an assumed name. He would think of the ruin he had brought upon his soul. But moments like these were rare. Dorian was still considered a respectable member of society. He threw lavish parties and attended formal dinners. He set trends by dressing in the finest clothes. He spent money on beautiful things including perfume, jewelry, and tapestries. He lived his life carelessly and spent his money recklessly.

But all these treasures were a means of escape. In that lonely, locked room was the portrait whose changing features showed him the real corruption of his life.

For weeks he would not go to the nursery. He wanted to forget the hideous thing and go back to his old life. Then suddenly, some nights he would creep out of the house and go down to horribly dreadful places near Blue Gate Fields. He'd stay there day after day, until he was driven away. On his return he would sit in front of the picture, hating it and himself.

As the years passed, Dorian continued to watch his painted image decay. He hated to be separated from it. And even though there were bars on the locked door, he worried that someone might break in and steal the portrait. Then everyone would know his secret! Perhaps the world suspected already.

Yes, there were people who distrusted him. He was nearly blackballed at the West

End Club. Once, when he was brought in by a friend, the Duke of Berwick and another gentleman walked out in a huff.

Just after his twenty-fifth birthday, it was rumored that he had been seen fighting with foreign sailors and consorting with thieves.

His long absences became well known. When he'd return to society, men would whisper to each other in corners. They would sneer as they walked past or look at him with cold, searching eyes. It was as though they were determined to discover his secret.

Dorian had been poisoned by Lord Henry's book. But to him, the evil was beautiful.

A Confrontation

Many years passed. On November ninth, the night before Dorian's thirty-eighth birthday, he was walking home at about eleven o'clock. Since the evening was so cold and foggy, he was wrapped in a heavy fur coat.

At the corner of Grosvenor Square and South Audley Street, a man passed him in the mist. The man's collar was turned up and he held a bag in his hand. Dorian recognized him. It was Basil Hallward. A strange sense of fear came over him, but he wasn't sure why. It seemed Basil had not noticed him, so he hurried on in the direction of his house.

But Basil had seen him. Dorian heard him stop, then hurry after him. In a few moments Basil's hand was on his arm.

"Dorian! What an extraordinary piece of luck! I have been waiting for you in your library since nine o'clock. Finally I took pity on your tired servant and left so he could go to bed. I am going to Paris on the midnight train, and I really wanted to see you before I left. I realized it was you as I passed. Didn't you recognize me?"

"In this fog, Basil?" Dorian replied. "I barely recognize the street. I'm not even sure where my house is. But I am sorry you're going away. I haven't seen you in ages. Will you be back soon?"

"No, I'll be away for six months. I intend to open a studio in Paris. I have an idea for a picture, and I want to shut myself away until it is completed. But I'm not here to talk about me. Let's go into your house. I have something to tell you."

"But won't you miss your train?" Dorian asked as he unlocked his door.

Basil looked at his watch. "I have heaps of time," he answered. "The train doesn't leave till twelve fifteen. It's only eleven."

Basil followed Dorian through his house and into the library, where a bright wood fire blazed in the large, open hearth.

"I want to speak to you seriously, Dorian. And don't frown like that. You make it more difficult for me," Basil said.

"What is it about?" Dorian asked, flinging himself down on the sofa.

"It's about you," Basil answered in a grave, deep voice. "I think you should know that some dreadful things are being said about you in London."

"I don't want to hear them," Dorian said. "I love scandals about other people, but scandals about myself are boring."

"You should hear them. Of course I don't believe any of these rumors at all. Especially when I see you. But they are saying the most horrible things about you. That you sneak around at night, going into terrible places and befriending the worst kinds of people. It seems gossip and shame follow you wherever you go."

"Don't concern yourself, Basil."

"Don't concern myself? Dorian, do I even know you anymore? I guess before I could answer that I would have to see your soul."

"To see my soul!" Dorian said, startling up from the couch, white with fear. A bitter laugh broke from his lips. "You shall see it tonight!" he cried, seizing a lamp from the table. "Come see your handiwork. There's no reason you shouldn't see it. Even if you tell the world about it afterward, nobody would believe you."

"I will come with you if you wish it. All I want is a plain answer to my question," Basil said.

Dorian smiled, pointing up. "The answer is locked away."

Dorian walked out of the room and up the stairs. Basil followed close behind. The lamp cast fantastic shadows on the walls and staircase. A rising wind made some of the windows rattle.

When they reached the top of the landing, Dorian set the lamp down on the floor and took out the key.

"You still insist on knowing, Basil?" he asked as he turned the key.

"Yes."

"I am delighted," he answered, smiling. Then he added harshly, "You are the only man in the world who is entitled to know everything about me."

He opened the door and went in. A cold current of air passed them, and the light shot up for a moment in a flame of murky orange. Dorian shuddered.

"Shut the door behind you," he whispered as he placed the lamp on the table.

CHAPTER 10

An Alibi

Basil glanced around him with a puzzled expression. The room looked as if it had not been lived in for years. The whole place was covered in dust and the carpet was full of holes. There was a damp odor of mildew in the air.

"Draw back the curtain, Basil," Dorian said in a cold, cruel voice.

"You are mad, Dorian."

"If you won't do it, then I'll have to do it myself." Dorian tore the curtain from its rod and flung it on the ground.

An exclamation of horror broke from Basil's lips as he saw the hideous face on the canvas grinning at him.

Good heavens! It was Dorian's own face that he was looking at. But was this the same

painting? He recognized his own brushwork, and the frame was the one he'd designed. He seized a candle and held it to the picture. In the left-hand corner was his own name.

He felt as if his blood had changed from fire to sluggish ice. Why had it been altered? He turned and looked at Dorian with the eyes of a sick man.

Dorian was leaning against the mantel, watching him with a strange expression.

"What does this mean?" Basil cried.

"Don't you remember? Years ago when I was a boy, you met me, flattered me. You introduced me to Henry, who taught me to treasure my good looks. In a mad moment, I made a wish. Perhaps you remember it."

"Oh, how well I remember it! No! It's impossible," Basil proclaimed.

Dorian walked over to the window and leaned his forehead against the cold glass. "Ah, what is impossible?"

"I don't believe it's my picture. This portrait has the eyes of a devil!"

"Basil, this is my soul."

"Then you have done much evil in your life. Don't you see the thing leering at us?"

Basil threw himself into a rickety chair that was standing by the table. He buried his face in his hands.

Dorian glanced at the picture. He suddenly felt an uncontrollable hatred for Basil. It was as though the image in the picture whispered in his ear. The mad passions of a cornered animal stirred within him. Dorian hated Basil more than anything in his whole life.

Dorian glanced around wildly. His eye fell on a knife that glimmered on the top of a chest. He moved slowly toward it, sneaking by Basil. As soon as he was behind Basil, Dorian seized the knife and turned around.

Basil stirred in his chair as if he was going to rise. Dorian rushed at him and dug the knife into his neck, crushing the man's head down on the table and stabbing him again and again.

Basil groaned. Three times he reached up, waving his stiff-fingered hands in the air. Dorian stabbed him twice more. Something began to trickle on the floor. Dorian waited a moment, still pressing Basil's head down. Then he threw the knife on the table and listened.

He could hear nothing but the *drip, drip* of blood on the thin carpet. He opened the door and went out on the landing. The house was absolutely quiet. For a few seconds, he stood peering down into the darkness. Then he returned to the room, locking himself inside.

How quickly it had all been done! Dorian felt strangely calm. He walked over to the window, opened it, and stepped out onto the balcony. The wind had blown the fog away, and he saw a policeman going about his rounds. A woman in a fluttering shawl was creeping slowly along, staggering as she went.

A bitter blast swept across the square. The gas lamps flickered. The leafless trees shook their branches to and fro. Dorian shivered and closed the window behind him.

He hurried to the door and turned the key. He did not even glance at the murdered man. The friend who had painted the fatal portrait had gone out of his life. That was enough.

Having locked the door, he quietly crept down the creaky stairs. When he reached the library, he saw Basil's bag and coat. He hid them away, sat down, and began to think.

What evidence was there against him? Basil

had left the house at eleven. No one had seen him come in again. And Basil was scheduled to go to Paris by train. It would be months before anyone knew he was missing. Months!

A sudden thought struck him. He needed an alibi. He put on his coat and hat and went outside. Then he began ringing his doorbell. In about five minutes, his valet answered the door, half dressed and looking very drowsy.

"I am sorry to wake you, Francis," he said, stepping in, "but I seem to have forgotten my key. What time is it?"

"Ten minutes past two, sir," answered the man, looking at the clock and blinking.

"Ten minutes past two? How horribly late! Did anyone call this evening?" Dorian asked.

"Mr. Hallward, sir. He stayed here till eleven."

"Did he leave any message?"

"Only that he'd write to you from Paris."

"Thank you, Francis. That will be all. Please wake me at nine o'clock in the morning."

CHAPTER 11

PANIC

At nine o'clock the next morning, Dorian's servant came in with a cup of hot chocolate and opened the shutters. Dorian was sleeping quite peacefully. He looked like a boy who'd been tired from playing too hard. The man had to touch him twice on the shoulder to wake him.

Dorian turned around and, leaning on his elbow, began to sip his chocolate. The mellow November sun came streaming into the room. The sky was bright and warm. It was almost like a morning in May.

Gradually the events of the preceding night crept into his brain. He winced at the memory of what he had done, and for a moment he felt the same hatred for Basil as he had the night before. And the dead man was still sitting there in his house!

After finishing his drink, Dorian sat down at a table and wrote two letters. One he put in his pocket, the other he handed to the valet.

"Take this round to 152 Hertford Street, Francis. Deliver it to Mr. Campbell. I must see him."

Dorian waited, stretching out on a sofa and reading. But he grew nervous. What if Alan Campbell was out of the country? What if he refused to come? What would he do then? Every moment was of vital importance. They had been close friends five years ago. But things were different now.

Alan Campbell was an extremely clever young man who loved chemistry. At Cambridge, he had spent a great deal of his time working in the laboratory. He was also an excellent musician. He played both the violin and the piano. In fact, it was music that had first brought him and Dorian together.

Whether or not a quarrel had taken place between them, no one ever knew. They scarcely spoke when they met, and Campbell always left a party when Dorian showed up. He had changed, too—giving up music and absorbing himself in his scientific research.

Dorian kept glancing at the clock. He got up and began to pace around the room like a caged animal. His hands were extremely cold.

The suspense was unbearable. Time seemed to be crawling with lead feet. The more he waited, the more frightened he became. His imagination ran wild, filling him with horror.

At last the door opened and his servant entered. He turned glazed eyes upon him.

"Mr. Campbell, sir," the servant said.

Dorian breathed a sigh of relief, and the color returned to his cheeks. "Ask him to come in at once, Francis." He felt that he was himself again. His cowardly mood had passed.

The servant bowed. In a few moments Alan Campbell walked in, looking stern and pale.

"Alan! This is kind of you! Thank you for coming," Dorian said to his guest.

"I had intended to never enter your house again, Gray. But you said it was a matter of life and death." He spoke slowly, his voice was hard and cold. He glared at Dorian.

"Yes, it is a matter of life and death. Sit down."

Alan chose a chair by the table. Dorian sat opposite to him. The two men's eyes met. Dorian knew that what he was going to do was dreadful.

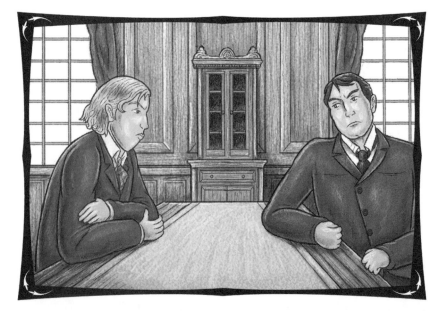

ALAN CAMPBELL

After a strained silence, Dorian leaned across and said, "Alan, in a locked room at the top of this house, a dead man is seated at a table. He has been dead ten hours now. Who the man is and why and how he died, doesn't concern you. What you have to do is this—"

"Stop, Gray. I don't want to know anything further. Whether what you told me is true or not doesn't concern me. I won't be mixed up in this. Keep your horrible secrets to yourself. They don't interest me anymore."

"Alan, they will have to interest you. I am sorry to do this, but I can't help myself. You are the one man who is able to save me. I am forced to bring you into this matter. I have no other option."

Dorian continued, "You know so much about science and chemistry. You have done experiments. I need you to destroy the thing upstairs. Nobody saw this person come into the house. Right now he is supposed to be in Paris. He will not be missed for months. When he is missed, there must be no trace of him.

"You, Alan, must change him and everything that belongs to him. Turn it all into a handful of ashes that can be scattered in the wind."

"You are mad, Dorian," Alan said. "You are mad to think that I would raise a finger to help you. Do you think I am going to risk my reputation for you? It doesn't matter to me what you are up to."

"It was suicide, Alan."

"I'm glad to hear that. But you are probably the one who drove him to it."

"Do you still refuse to do this for me?"

"Of course I refuse. How dare you ask me to get mixed up in this horror? You have come to the wrong man," Alan said.

"Alan, it was murder," Dorian confessed. "I killed him. He had made me suffer. My life is terrible because of him."

"Murder! Is that what you have come to? Don't worry, I won't inform the police. All criminals eventually do something stupid and get caught. I'm sure you will, too. So I will have nothing to do with it."

"Listen to me, Alan. Just listen," Dorian said. "All I ask is that you perform a certain scientific experiment. You have spent time in hospitals and morgues, and the horrors there don't affect you. If you had found this man in a laboratory or on a dissecting table, you would simply look at him as a medical subject.

"As a matter of fact, you would think the experiment would be something that would benefit the human race. To destroy a body is far less horrible than what you are accustomed to. And remember, it is the only piece of evidence against me. If it is discovered, I am lost. It is sure to be discovered if you don't help me."

"I have no desire to help you," Alan insisted.

"Alan, please. Look at it from a scientific point of view. You don't ask about the dead bodies that are subjects of your experiments. Please don't ask now. But I beg you to do this. We were friends once, Alan."

"Don't speak to me of those days, Dorian."

"Alan, the man upstairs will not go away. He is sitting at the table with his head bowed. Alan! Alan! If you don't help me I am ruined. They will hang me for what I have done."

"I refuse. It is insane of you to ask me."

Dorian looked at Alan with pity in his eyes. He stretched out his hand, took a piece of paper, and wrote something on it. He folded it carefully and pushed it across the table. Then he got up and went to the window.

Campbell looked at him in surprise. He took up the paper and opened it. As he read it, his face became ghastly pale. A horrible sense of sickness came over him. He felt as if his heart was beating itself to death.

THE END OF A FRIENDSHIP

After two or three minutes of silence had passed, Dorian turned around. He came over and stood behind Alan, putting his hand upon his shoulder.

"I am so sorry for you, Alan," he murmured, "but you leave me no choice. I have a letter written already. Here it is. You see the address. If you don't help me, I will send it. You know what the results will be. But you are going to help me. It would be impossible for you to refuse now."

Alan buried his face in his hands. A shudder passed through him.

"Don't worry so much, Alan. The thing has to be done. Face it, and do it."

A groan broke from Alan's lips, and he shivered all over. He felt as if an iron ring was slowly being tightened around his forehead.

"Come, Alan, you must do it," Dorian repeated.

Alan hesitated a moment, then asked, "Is there a fire in the room upstairs?"

"Yes, there is a gas fire."

"I shall have to go home and get some things from the laboratory."

"No, Alan, you must not leave the house. Write out what you want on a sheet of notepaper. My servant will go and bring the things back to you."

Campbell scrawled out what he needed. Dorian took the note up and read it carefully. Then he rang the bell and gave it to his valet. He told him to return as soon as possible with the things.

Alan got up from his chair and went over to the fireplace. For nearly twenty minutes, neither man spoke. A fly buzzed noisily about the room, and the ticking of the clock was like the beat of a hammer.

As the clock struck one, Alan turned around to see that Dorian's eyes were filled with tears. "You have saved my life," Dorian said.

"Dorian, you have lived a life of corruption, and now you have committed murder. I am doing this because you are forcing me. It is not your life that I am thinking about."

After about ten minutes, there was a knock at the door. The servant entered, carrying a large chest filled with chemicals. Once they were delivered, Dorian sent the servant away for the evening.

"Now, Alan, there is not a moment to lose. Let me carry the chest up for you." When they reached the room, Dorian took out the key and turned it in the lock. Then he stopped and a troubled look came into his eyes. He shuddered.

"I don't think I can go in," he murmured.

"It doesn't matter. I don't need your help," said Alan, coldly.

Dorian half-opened the door. As he did, he saw the face of his portrait leering in the sunlight. The cloth was lying on the floor in front of it. He had forgotten to cover it. He was about to rush forward when he drew back with a shudder. What was that ghastly red dew on one of the hands? It looked like the canvas had sweated blood. How horrible it was!

He took a deep breath and opened the door a little wider. He half-closed his eyes and turned his head so he couldn't see the dead man. Then, swooping down, he picked up the gold-and-purple cloth and flung it over the picture.

Dorian heard Alan bringing in the heavy chest. "Leave me now," Alan said in a stern voice. Dorian hurried back down the stairs.

It was long after seven when Alan came back into the library. He was pale but calm. "I have done what you asked me to do," he muttered. "And now I never want to see you again."

TRYING TO ESCAPE

Dorian hailed a hansom cab and gave the driver the address. "Drive quickly!" Dorian ordered. "You must hurry!"

A cold rain began to fall. The blurred street lamps looked ghastly in the mist. The public houses were closing, and men and women clustered in broken groups around their doors. From the bars came the sound of horrible laughter as drunken men brawled and shouted.

Lying back in the seat, with his hat pulled down over his forehead, Dorian watched the shame of the great city. He repeated to himself something Lord Henry had said on the first day they met.

"To cure the soul by means of the senses, and the senses by means of the soul."

Yes, that was the secret.

There were opium dens where men could drown their sorrows. Dorian had done it before. He would do it again to erase the memory of murdering Basil.

The moon hung low in the sky like a yellow skull. From time to time a huge, thin cloud stretched across, hiding it. Soon the gas lamps grew fewer and the streets more narrow and gloomy. The hideous hunger for opium gnawed at him. His throat burned and his hands twitched.

Suddenly the driver jerked to a halt at the top of a dark lane. Over the low roofs and jagged chimneys rose the black masts of ships. Wreaths of white mist clung like ghostly sails to the shipyards.

"Somewhere about here, sir, ain't it?" the driver asked, huskily.

Dorian peered around. "This will do," he answered.

Dorian got out hastily and gave the driver some extra coins. Then he walked quickly in the direction of the docks. Here and there a merchant's lantern gleamed. A red glare came from an outbound coal ship. And the slimy pavement looked like a wet raincoat.

He hurried on to the left, glancing back now and then to see if he was being followed. In about seven or eight minutes he reached a small, shabby house that was wedged between two bleak factories. In one of the top windows stood a lamp. Dorian stopped and knocked on the door.

After a little time, he heard steps and the sound of the chain being unhooked. The door opened quietly. He went in without saying a word to the man standing in the shadow. At the end of the hall hung a tattered green curtain. He dragged it aside and entered a long, low room.

In one corner a drunken sailor was sprawled over a table, his head buried in his arms. Two women at the bar were laughing and drinking as Dorian passed by

At the end of the room there was a little staircase leading up to a dark chamber. Dorian could smell the heavy odor of opium as he hurried up the rickety steps. When he entered, a yellow-haired man, who was bending over a lamp, looked up at him.

"You are here, Adrian?" muttered Dorian.

"Where else would I be?" he answered slowly. "Because of you, no one will speak to me anymore."

Dorian remembered that Basil had spoken of Adrian's ruin. And Dorian was to blame for this man's pitiful condition.

"I thought you left England," Dorian said.

"I'm right here, Dorian. And I don't care anymore," he added with a sigh. "As long as I have this stuff, I don't need friends."

Dorian winced and looked around him. People were lying on ragged mattresses, their limbs twisted and their mouths gaping. They stared off with dull, cloudy eyes.

Dorian knew how they suffered. He was imprisoned by the thought of Basil Hallward. It was eating away at his soul. He needed opium to escape the memory, but the presence of Adrian Singleton troubled him.

"I'm going to another place," he said, after a pause.

Dorian walked to the door with a look of pain on his face. A hideous laugh broke from the painted lips of a woman at the bar. She snapped her fingers and called out, "Prince Charming!"

PRINCE CHARMING

"That's what you like to be called, ain't it?" the woman yelled after him.

The drowsy sailor leaped to his feet as she spoke and looked wildly around. As Dorian shut the door, the man rushed out after him.

Dorian hurried along the docks in the drizzling rain. He wondered if he had ruined Adrian Singleton's life as Basil had said. He bit his lip, and for a few seconds his eyes grew sad. But it didn't matter. Each man lived his own life and paid his own price.

Dorian paced on, quickening his steps. He darted into a dim archway when someone seized him from behind. Before he had time to defend himself, he was thrust back against the wall. A brutal hand clutched his throat.

Dorian struggled madly to pull the tightening fingers away. In a second he heard the click of a revolver and saw the gleam of the polished barrel pointing straight at his head. The dark form of a stocky man faced him.

"What do you want?" Dorian gasped.

"Keep quiet," said the man. "If you stir, I'll shoot you."

"You are mad. What have I done to you?"

"You wrecked the life of Sibyl Vane," he answered, "and Sibyl Vane was my sister. She killed herself, and it was your fault. I swore I would kill you in return. For years I have searched for you. I had no clue, no trace. The two people who could describe you were dead. I knew nothing about you except the name she called you. And I heard it tonight. Make peace with your God, for tonight you are going to die."

Dorian grew sick with fear. "I never knew her," he stammered. "I've never heard of her. You are mad."

"You had better confess your sin, for as sure as I am James Vane, you are going to die."

There was a horrible moment when Dorian did not know what to say or do.

"Down on your knees!" growled the man. "I give you one minute to make your peace. I'm sailing to India tonight, and I must do my job first. One minute. That's all."

Dorian's arms fell to his side. Paralyzed with terror, he did not know what to do. Suddenly, a wild hope flashed across his brain.

"Stop!" he cried. "How long has it been since your sister died?"

"Eighteen years," said the man. "Why do you ask? What do years matter?"

"Eighteen years," laughed Dorian, with a touch of triumph in his voice. "Eighteen years! Set me under the street lamp and look at my face!"

James Vane hesitated for a moment. Then he seized Dorian and dragged him from the archway. The light was dim and wavering from the wind, but it showed him what a hideous mistake he was about to make. The man he was about to kill had the youthful face of a boy. He didn't look more than twenty years old. It was obvious that this was not the man who had destroyed his sister's life.

James loosened his hold and stumbled back. "My God!" he cried. "And I would have murdered you!"

Dorian Gray drew in a long breath. "You were on the edge of committing a terrible crime, my man," he said, looking at him sternly. "Let this be a warning to you not to take vengeance into your own hands."

"Forgive me, sir," muttered Vane. "I was deceived. Hearing that name confused me."

"You had better go home and put that pistol away, or you may get into trouble," said Dorian as he turned and walked slowly away.

Vane stood on the pavement in horror. He was trembling from head to foot. After a little while, a woman who had been drinking at the bar hurried to him.

"Why didn't you kill him?" she hissed, putting her haggard face close to his. "I knew you were following him when you rushed out. You fool! You should have killed him. He has lots of money and he's a bad fellow."

"He is not the man I am looking for," he answered. "And I want no man's money. I want a man's life. The man I hunt must be nearly forty now. This one is little more than a boy. Thank God I have not got his blood on my hands."

The woman gave a bitter laugh. "Little more than a boy!" she sneered. "Why, man, it's been eighteen years since I knew Prince Charming. He made me what I am."

"You lie!" cried Vane.

"I am telling the truth. He is the worst one that comes here. They say he sold himself to the devil for a pretty face. It's been eighteen years since I've met him, and he's barely changed."

"You swear this?"

"I swear it. But don't tell him I'm the one who told you," she whined. "I am afraid of him."

James made an oath to her that he wouldn't tell. Then he broke away and rushed to the corner of the street, but Dorian Gray had disappeared. When he looked back, the woman had vanished, too.

CHAPTER 16

A BAD OMEN

A week later, Dorian Gray was sitting in the conservatory at his country estate, talking to the pretty Duchess of Monmouth. Her husband, a weary-looking man of sixty, was seated among his guests. The house party consisted of twelve people, and more were expected to arrive the next day.

At dinner that evening, they ate and chattered. Dorian was a gracious host. His mind was on nothing but the dinner and all his lavish surroundings. He seemed once again like the old Dorian, the one who could charm everyone in his company.

But while they were dining, Dorian happened to glace toward the window. A chill of terror ran through him! James Vane was there, and his rough, weathered face was pressed against the glass, watching him.

The next day Dorian did not leave the house. He spent most of the time in his room, sick with terror. He feared dying, and thoughts of being hunted and trapped dominated him.

Whenever he closed his eyes, he could see the sailor's face peering through the misty glass. But maybe it had only been his imagination. If any stranger had been prowling around the house, he would have been seen by the servants. If footprints had been found in the flower beds, the gardeners would have reported it. Yes, it had only been his imagination. Sibyl Vane's brother had not come back to kill him. The man had sailed away to India. Dorian was safe. Besides, Sibyl's brother did not even know who he was. The mask of youth had saved him.

But if it was an illusion, how terrible it is to see fearful phantoms. How horrible would life be if he was always tormented by his past crimes? He had killed his friend! The memory of it played over and over in Dorian's mind. Each hideous detail came back to him in horror. Finally Dorian calmed himself. He was home and safe with a house full of guests.

It was three days before Dorian ventured out. There was something in the clear, pine-scented air of that winter morning that brought him joy. After breakfast, he walked with the Duchess for about an hour, then drove across the park to join a hunting party. He saw Sir Geoffrey, the Duchess's brother, emptying two cartridges from his gun.

"How is the hunting today?" Dorian asked.

"Not very good, Dorian. I think it will be better after lunch."

Dorian strolled along next to Sir Geoffrey. The crisp smell of the air and the colorful red and brown of the leaves filled him with joy. Suddenly there was rustling in the grass. A large hare with black-tipped ears bolted toward the thicket. Sir Geoffrey put his gun to his shoulder.

There was something about the graceful movement of the animal that charmed Dorian. He cried out, "Don't shoot it, Geoffrey. Let it live."

"What nonsense, Dorian!" laughed his companion. As the hare bounded for the thicket, Sir Geoffrey fired.

They heard two dreadful cries. One was the hare in pain. But much worse was the other. The cry of a man in agony.

"Good heavens! I hit someone!" exclaimed Sir Geoffrey. "What a fool the man was to get in front of the guns! Stop shooting there!" he called to the other hunters. "A man is hurt."

A groundskeeper came running up with a stick in his hand. "Where, sir? Where is he?" he shouted.

"Here," answered Sir Geoffrey, hurrying toward the thicket.

Dorian watched them as they plunged into the brush, swinging branches aside. In a few moments they emerged, dragging a body into the sunlight. He turned away in horror. He could not look.

"Is the man dead?" Sir Geoffrey asked the keeper.

"Yes, sir."

This is a bad omen, Dorian thought. *Bad luck follows me everywhere.*

Dorian spent the rest of the day inside, lying on a sofa and trembling with terror. Life had suddenly become such a burden. Death was all around him.

I'll leave, he thought. *I must get away from here at once.* But curiosity would not let him go. He had to know who the dead man was. Was he one of the groundsmen? Did he leave behind a family?

At five o'clock he sent for the head groundskeeper. "What do you know about the man who was shot?" Dorian asked him. "Who is he?"

"We don't know who he is, sir."

"Don't know who he is?" Dorian questioned. "What do you mean? Wasn't he one of the other groundsmen?"

"No, sir. Never saw him before. Looks like he might have been a sailor, sir."

Dorian felt as though his heart had suddenly stopped beating. "A sailor?" he cried out.

"Yes, sir. Both of his arms had tattoos, just like a sailor."

Dorian anxiously leaned forward. "What else can you tell me about him? Was there anything found with him?"

"Some money, sir. Not much though. And a six-shooter. He was a decent-looking man, but rough-like."

"Where is the body?" Dorian asked. "I must see it at once."

"In the empty stable," the keeper replied.

Dorian rushed out, mounted his horse, and galloped down the road as hard as he could.

When he reached the stable, he leaped from his horse and hurried to the door. He paused for a moment, then thrust the door open and entered.

In the corner lay the dead body of a man dressed in a coarse shirt and blue trousers. A handkerchief had been placed over his face. A candle, stuck in a bottle, flickered beside him.

Dorian shuddered. He walked slowly toward the body. He wasn't sure if he could do it, but he knelt down and carefully removed the handkerchief from the man's face. Dorian gasped. The man who had been shot in the thicket was James Vane!

He stood there for a few more minutes, looking at the dead body. As he rode home, his eyes filled with tears. James Vane was dead. And now Dorian knew that he was safe.

A NEW DORIAN

"There is no use in you telling me that you're going to be good!" cried Lord Henry. "You are already perfect. Please don't change."

Dorian shook his head. "No, Harry, I have done too many dreadful things in my life. I am not going to do anymore."

"My dear boy," said Lord Henry, smiling, "anybody can be good in the country. There are no temptations there. Country people have no opportunity to do harm."

"I have known good and bad," Dorian said. "But I want to be better. I am going to be better." Dorian paused. "But tell me, Harry. What's going on in town?"

Lord Henry sighed. "People are still talking about poor Basil's disappearance."

"I would have thought they'd be tired of that gossip by now," said Dorian, frowning slightly.

Lord Henry nodded. "They've been chattering about it for six weeks. But the British public loves a scandal. They've whispered about my own divorce and Alan Campbell's suicide. Now they've got the mysterious disappearance of the artist to occupy them.

"Scotland Yard still insists that a man resembling Basil left for Paris by the midnight train on the ninth of November. The French police declare that Basil never arrived in Paris at all."

"What do you think has happened to Basil?" asked Dorian, trying to stay calm.

"I have no idea. If Basil is hiding, it's none of my business."

Dorian rose and walked into the next room. He sat at the piano and let his fingers stray across the keys. "Harry, did it ever occur to you that Basil could have been murdered?"

Lord Henry yawned. "Basil was very popular. Why should he have been murdered? He had no enemies. When it came to art, the man was a genius. But Basil was rather dull."

"I was very fond of Basil," Dorian said, with a note of sadness in his voice. "But no one thinks he was murdered?"

"Oh, some of the newspapers do. But it doesn't seem likely to me. There are dreadful places in Paris, but Basil was not the sort of man to go to them," Lord Henry said.

"Harry, what would you say if I told you I had murdered Basil?"

"You are not the type to commit murder, Dorian. Crime is vulgar. Only the lower classes commit such terrible acts. It is not in you to commit murder. But let's talk about something else. I would like to think something good has happened to Basil, but knowing him, he probably fell into the river. And his artwork hasn't been very good in the last ten years. Not since he painted that portrait of you."

Dorian heaved a sigh, and Lord Henry strolled across the room.

"By the way," Lord Henry asked, "what became of the wonderful portrait? It was a masterpiece."

"I forget," Dorian said. "I never really liked it. The memory of it is hateful to me."

"But it was a wonderful likeness of you," Lord Henry said. "It captured your youth." Then he sat back and looked at Dorian with narrowed eyes. "Tell me, Dorian, how have you kept your youthful look? You must have some secret. I am ten years older than you, and I am wrinkled and worn. You still look the same as the day I met you. You are still the same."

"I am not the same, Harry."

"Yes, you are."

Dorian rose up from the piano and passed his hand through his hair. "You don't know everything about me, Harry. If you did, you'd never speak to me again."

"Never," said Lord Henry. "You and I will always be friends."

Dorian glared at him and sat nearby. "And yet you poisoned me with that book. I will never forgive you for that. Harry, promise me you will never lend that book to anyone else. It's harmful."

"My dear boy, you sound like a minister preaching about sin. You are much too delightful to do that. Besides, it is no use. You and I are what we are. And there is no such thing as being poisoned by a book. But enough about that. Meet me tomorrow. I will take you to lunch with Lady Branksome. She is a charming woman."

Dorian was reluctant. "Very well. I'll meet you at eleven. Good night, Harry."

The next night was so warm that Dorian threw his coat over his arm as he walked home from the Branksomes. He didn't even put his silk scarf around his neck.

As he strolled home, two nicely dressed young men passed him. "That is Dorian Gray," one of them whispered to the other. Dorian used to love being pointed out, stared at, or talked about. But now he was tired of hearing his own name. Half the charm of the little village where he had been so often lately was that no one knew who he was.

When he reached home, he found his servant waiting up for him. He sent him away and threw himself down on the sofa in the library.

He began to think over some of the things that Lord Henry had said to him.

Was it really true that a person could never change? He felt a wild longing to be as innocent as when he was a boy. He knew that it was his own fault that he was a tarnished man. He had been an evil influence on others and had enjoyed it. But that couldn't be reversed. Dorian wondered, *Is there no hope for me now?*

Ah! It was in that monstrous moment of pride and passion when he prayed that the portrait would bear his burdens, and he would always stay young. All his failures had been due to that.

Dorian picked up the mirror that he'd used so many years ago to compare his face to the one in the portrait. He looked into it with tear-rimmed eyes. Hating his own beauty, he flung the mirror onto the floor and crushed it into silver splinters with his heel. It was his beauty that had ruined him. His youth had spoiled him.

It was better not to think of the past. Nothing could change that. He had to think of himself and his own future. James Vane was hidden in a nameless grave back in the country churchyard. Alan Campbell had shot himself one night in his laboratory but had not revealed the secret Dorian had forced upon him. The excitement over Basil Hallward's disappearance would soon pass away. It was already dying out. Dorian was perfectly safe.

But it was Basil's death that weighed upon his mind. And the living death of his own soul troubled him. Basil had painted the portrait that had scarred his life. He could not forgive him for that. It was the portrait that had done everything. The murder had been simply the madness of the moment. As for Alan Campbell's suicide, that had been his own act. He had chosen to do it. That had nothing to do with Dorian.

A new life! That was what he wanted. That was what he was waiting for. And it had begun already. He would never again be tempted to do evil. He would be good.

Dorian began to wonder if the portrait in the locked room had changed. Surely it was not still as horrible as it had been? Maybe if his life became pure, he would be able to erase every sign of evil passion from the face. Maybe the signs of evil had already gone away. He would go and look.

He took the lamp from the table and crept upstairs. As he unlocked the door, a smile of joy flitted across his youthful face and lingered for a moment on his lips.

Yes, he would be good, and the hideous thing that he had hidden away would no longer be a terror to him. He felt as if a load had been lifted from him already.

Dorian went in quietly, locking the door behind him.

DESTROYING THE PORTRAIT

Dorian stepped up to the portrait, hesitated, then dragged the purple hanging away. A cry of pain and hatred broke from him. He could not see any change. There was a devious look in the eyes, and the mouth was twisted into an evil sneer. The scarlet dew that had spotted the hand seemed brighter now. It looked like newly spilled blood.

Dorian trembled. Why was the horrid stain larger? There was blood at the painted feet, as though the thing had dripped. There was even blood on the hand that had not held the knife.

Did this mean he should confess his sins? Was he to give himself up and be put to death? He laughed. He felt that the idea was monstrous. Besides, even if he did confess, who would believe him? There was no trace of the murdered man anywhere. He, himself, had burned Basil's things downstairs. The world would simply say that he was mad. They would lock him in a mental institution if he shared his story.

Yet, it was his duty to confess and suffer public shame. Confessing was the only thing that would cleanse him of his horrible deeds. Dorian gazed at the portrait. It was the mirror of his soul he was looking at. He had tried to deny it, but he recognized it now.

But would Basil's murder haunt him all of his life? Would he always be burdened by the past? Should he confess? Never.

There was only one bit of evidence against him. The picture itself. He would destroy it. Why had he kept it so long? It used to give him pleasure to watch it change and grow old. But lately, he had felt no pleasure. It had kept him awake at night. And when he was away, he was filled with terror that someone might come in and see it. Yes, he would destroy it.

He looked around and saw the knife he had used to stab Basil. He had cleaned it many times, and there were no stains left on it. It was bright and glistening. And just as it had killed the painter, it would kill the painter's work. When that was dead, then he would be free. It would kill this monstrous soul, and he would be at peace. He seized the knife and stabbed the picture with it.

There was a loud cry and a crash. The agony of the cry was so horrible that the frightened servants woke and crept out of their rooms. Two gentlemen who were passing the square below stopped and looked up at the great house. They hurried on until they found a policeman and brought him back. The men rang the bell several times, but there was no answer. Except for a light in one of the top windows, the house was dark. After a time, they stood back and watched.

"Whose house it that, constable?" asked one of the gentlemen.

"Mr. Dorian Gray's," answered the policeman. The two men sneered and walked away.

Inside the house, the servants scurried about in their nightclothes, whispering to each other. Old Mrs. Leaf was crying and wringing her hands. Francis was as pale as death.

After waiting about fifteen minutes, Francis, the coachman, and one of the footmen crept up quietly and knocked on the door. There was no reply. They tried and tried to force the door open, but it would not budge. Finally, they crawled up on the roof and dropped down onto the balcony. The windows opened easily since the bolts were old.

When they entered, they found the splendid portrait of their master hanging on the wall. It looked just as it had when they last saw it, displaying Dorian's flawless beauty and youth.

But on the floor was a dead man with a knife stabbed in his heart. He was withered and wrinkled. His face looked worn and beastly.

"Who do you think it is?" the coachman asked.

Francis shook his head. He leaned down to examine the body. He didn't recognize the man at all until—"His rings!" he cried. "Look at his rings!" They were indeed those of his master.

They were never able to explain what happened. They never knew the truth. Dorian had not succeeded in destroying the picture. He only succeeded in changing places with it. He had at last destroyed himself.